Little Treasures

Little Treasures

Endearments from Around the World

words by Jacqueline K. Ogburn

pictures by Chris Raschka

Houghton Mifflin Books for Children

Houghton Mifflin Harcourt

Boston New York 2011

Houghton Mifflin Books for Children is an imprint of Houghton Mifflin Harcourt Publishing Company.

www.hmhbooks.com

The text of this book is set in Magma Halo with hand-lettering by the artist.
The illustrations are ink, watercolor, and gouache.
Book design by Carol Goldenberg

Library of Congress Cataloging-in-Publication Data
Ogburn, Jacqueline K.
Little treaures : endearments from around the world / written by Jacqueline Ogburn ; illustrated by Chris Raschka.
p. cm.
ISBN 978-0-547-42862-8
1. Children—Quotations. 2. Childhood—Quotations, maxims, etc. I. Raschka, Christopher. II. Title.
PN6084.C5O33 2011
808.88'2—dc22
2010044362

Manufactured in Singapore
TWP 10 9 8 7 6 5 4 3 2 1

4500322579

To my daughters, my sweetie girls,
Claire and Emily Deahl

—J.K.O.

～～～～～

For my Schätzchen

—C.R.

Does your mother call you silly things such as "sweetheart" or "doodlebug"? Does your father call you "peanut" or "short stuff"? These kinds of sweet and silly names are known as endearments.

All over the world, mothers and fathers, grandparents and cousins, brothers and sisters, uncles and aunts, love their children very much and call them by many different sweet names.

English-speaking people love their children very much.

In America, they call their children

honey

sunshine

pumpkin

and baby-cakes.

In England, people call their children sweet names such as

poppet   pet   ducky   and love.

In Australia, families call their children

flossie

possum

and lambchop.

French-speaking mothers and fathers, grandparents and cousins, sisters and brothers, uncles and aunts, love their children very much and call them

my darling	my rabbit	my flea	and my little cabbage.

ma chérie	mon lapin	ma puce	mon petit chou
(mah shay-REE)	(mon la-PAN)	(mah POOss)	(mon pe-TI SHOO)

In Finland, families use endearments such as

and flower bud.

star eye

hug bunny

nugget of gold

kullanmuru
(KU-llan-MU-ru)

tahtisilma
(TAH-ti-sil-MA)

halipupu
(HA-li-pu-pu)

nuppunen
(NU-pu-nen)

sunny sun Солнышко

Russian-speaking people call their children sweet names such as

solnyshko
(SOL-nysh-kah)

little paw
лапочка

precious or golden one
золотой

zolotoi
(zah-lah-TO-ye)

and dumpling.
карапуз

lapochka
(LAH-pah-chka)

karapuz
(kah-rah-POOZ)

In Poland, where mothers and fathers and grandparents and cousins love their children very much, those children are called

little mouse

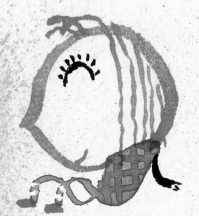

bear cub

happiness

and little sun.

myszka
(MI-shka)

misiaczk
(mi-shi-ACHK)

szczescie
(SHCHAIN-shchyea)

słoneczko
(swon-ECH-ko)

In Uganda, where Lugandan-speaking parents love their children very much,
they use endearments such as

sweetheart   princess   and pampered one.

mukwano
(mu-KWAN-o)

mumbejja
(mum-BEY-ja)

kabiite
(ka-BEE-tay)

Portuguese-speaking people love their children very much,
and in Brazil they call their children sweet names such as

little coconut candy   cutie   and little love.

docinho de coco
(dos-IN-yo gee kO-ko)

fofinho
(fof-IN-yo)

amorzinho
(amor-ZIN-yo)

Arabic-speaking families love their children very much and call them

a part of my existence

ضنايا

dhanaya
(DAN-a-ya)

honey

عسل

asal
(ah-SAL)

beloved

حبيبي

habibi
(ha-BIBI-ti)

and light of my heart.

نور قلبي

noor khalbi
(NUR QAL-bi)

Chinese-speaking people love their children very much, and in Mandarin they call their children sweet names such as

precious or treasure
宝贝

bao bei
(BOW BAY)

little
mischevious pea
小皮豆

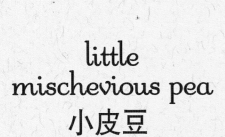

good child
乖乖

and most beloved.
心肝

xiao pie dou
(SHAO PI DOH)

guai guai
(KWAI KWAI)

xin gan
(SHIN GAN)

German-speaking families love their children very much and call them

treasure

Schatzi
(SHAT-see)

little kiss

Butzilein
(BU-se-LINE)

little mouse

kleine Maus
(KLI-na mouse)

and little
huggy bear.

Knuddelbaerchen
(KNU-del-BEAR-shen)

Hindi-speaking parents, grandparents, uncles, and aunts love their children very much and call them sweet names such as

my ruby
मेरा लाल

mera lal
(ME-ra LAL)

my babydoll
मेरा गुड्डा

mera gudda
(ME-ra GUD-da)

my princess
मेरी रानी

meri rani
(ME-ri RA-ni)

and my sweet little moon.
मेरा चंदा

mera chanda
(ME-ra CHAN-da)

In Ethiopia, Amharic-speaking people love their children very much,
and parents call their children

my beauty

my bubble of joy

and my berry.

yeinay qonjo
(YEN-ay KWON-jo)

yeinay filiklik
(YEN-ay FA-lik-lik)

yeinay injory
(YEN-ay en-JO-re)

In the Slovak Republic, parents call their children sweet names such as

golden one   little beetle   my heart   and my everything.

zlatko
(ZLAT-ko)

chrobáčik
(HRO-baa-chik)

srdiečko
(SIR-dee-ech-ko)

moje všetko
(MOY-ye VSHET-ko)

Spanish-speaking mothers and fathers, grandparents and cousins, brothers and sisters, uncles and aunts, love their children very much and call them by many, many endearments.

In Chile, families call their children sweet names such as

my chick	little piece of Heaven	little fatty	and little angel.
mi pollita	pedacito de cielo	gordito	angelito
(mee poh-YEE-tah)	(pay-dah-SEE-toh de see-AY-loh)	(gor-DEE-toh)	(an-je-LEE-toh)

In Argentina, parents also call their children

my little dear

mi cariñito
(mee kah-ree-NYEE-toh)

little candy

caramelito
(kah-rah-may-LEE-toh)

and little heart.

corazoncito
(koh-rah-zon-SEE-toh)

No matter where they live
or what language they speak,
all around the world families love
their children very much and use many
different endearments. All those mothers,
fathers, grandparents, cousins, brothers,
sisters, aunts, and uncles, whether
they say "sweetie pie," "mera chanda,"
"angelito," or use their own special
sweet names, they all are saying the
same thing: "I love you, child."

Acknowledgments

This book would not have been possible without the kindness of my friends and their friends. First and foremost is my editor, Kate O'Sullivan, who loved the idea from the start and helped find many of the endearments included through her international array of authors and illustrators. Her sister, Meghan O'Sullivan, professor of International Affairs at Harvard's Kennedy School of Government, also sent out the call and sent me the answers.

Since I live in Durham, I was also fortunate enough to have the help of many people at Duke University. Professor Edna Andrews, director of the Center for Slavic, Eurasian, and East European Languages, created pronunciations for the endearments, a task that was more drawn out than she had anticipated. Associate Dean Norman Keul, a linguist, read over the manuscript and made great suggestions and corrections. Margaret Riley, associate dean and director of Global Education, also put out the word for me several times over the years.

The following people also contributed in many ways, by sending endearments, translations, transcriptions, recordings, and endearments in other alphabets, by checking usage and spelling, or by referring me to their friends, who were happy to help a stranger. A special thank-you to Satti Khanna, who called this project "a tenderness mantra."

Abdulwahab Abdulla Al-Hajjri · Holly Ackeman · Howard Anderson · Kurt Amend · Edna Andrews
Emrakeb Assefa · Jeff Beal · Marc Bellemare · Tzvetan Benov · Pablo Bernasconi · Nic Bishop
Laurie Bley · Yanitzia Canett · Nicoletta Ceccoli · Catia Chien · Amy E. Cunningham · Ben Deahl
Claire Deahl · Linda Daniels · Alesha Daughtrey · Christine Davenier · David Ehrmann
Fabiola Estrada · Lukas Fischer · Lisa Finneran · Guilherme Gama · Lisa Giragosian · Carol Goldenberg
Elise Goldwasser · Srikanthi Gunturi · Kenzie Jackson · Monica Stubbs Jarnagin · Maggie Kao
Emmanuel Katongole · Norman Keul · Satti Khanna · Judith Kelley · Tom Keon · Katya Kolya
Tiina Laakkonen · Alexandra Lane · Renata Liwska · Avinash Maheshwary · Kibret Markos
Sheila Makindara · Mary Anne McDonald · Margaret Anne Miles · Patrick Morrison · Viwe Mtshontshi
Leah Niederstadt · Kate O'Sullivan · Meghan O'Sullivan · Anne Pa · Evian Patterson · Thomas Patterson
Charles Piot · Maarit Pokkinen · April Prince · Pamela G. Quanrud · Roula Qubain · Chris Raschka
Ben Redlich · Charlene Reiss · Ann Rider · Margaret Riley · James Rumford · Annika Sarin · Jennifer Salamh
Allen Say · Dan Schallau · Sebastia Serra · Samuel Silvers · Carmen Soza del Rio · Mark Svendsen
Yoko Tanaka · Barbara Thiede · Ralf Thiede · Miron Tequame · Donna Washington · Mary Wilcox
Tamara Wittes · Erica Zappy · Ernest A. Zitser · Luo Zhou

About the Book

This book includes only a fraction of the world's languages and endearments. At publication, most sources list Mandarin Chinese, Spanish, and English as the most commonly spoken languages. After English, Spanish is the most common language spoken in America, so I included more of those endearments.

The selection of the other languages was more arbitrary, depending on what I have been able to collect and verify. Fourteen languages worked well with the picture book format, so I tried for a range of languages and geography.

While endearments are common, they are not quite universal in the way Americans use them. Multiple sources told me that endearments are rarely used in Japanese. For the African languages, several sources told me of the practice of using kinship terms as endearments, such as parents calling their daughters "mother" or their sons "father." This seemed too complicated for this format, but I felt the book would be incomplete without an African tribal language, so I was happy I was able to include Lugandan, a member of the Bantu family of languages.

Even within a language there are regional differences in usage. The Portuguese terms were from Brazilian sources, so they many not be common in Portugal.

Many of these endearments are also used between lovers as well as between parents and children. For instance, for the Arabic terms *dyhanaya* and *asal,* sources from Egypt and Yemen reported their use with children, but in Jordan, they are used between lovers.

The pronunciations are simplified so readers can try to say all these sweet, beautiful words people use to express love for their children.

Many languages have a gender for nouns and adjectives, so I have tried to use a mix when possible. The gender, spelling, and pronunciation may change given how it is used, but generally I chose the most common form.

As always, exact translation is difficult. Endearments are a matter of usage, not strict definition. While I had all the endearments checked and vetted, any errors that persist are my own.